LIMITED EDITION

COPY NUMBER 140 OF 400

Chants of Freedom

Chants of Freedom
Poems Written in Exile

Mathews Phosa

PENGUIN BOOKS

Published by Penguin Books
an imprint of Penguin Random House South Africa (Pty) Ltd
Reg. No. 1953/000441/07
The Estuaries No. 4, Oxbow Crescent, Century Avenue,
Century City, 7441
PO Box 1144, Cape Town, 8000, South Africa

www.penguinbooks.co.za

First published 2015

1 3 5 7 9 10 8 6 4 2

Publication © Penguin Random House 2015
Text © Mathews Phosa 2015

Cover design: Monique Cleghorn

Set in 11 pt on 13.5 pt Adobe Caslon

Printed and bound by DJE Flexible Print Solutions

ISBN 978 1 4152 0776 5 (print)
ISBN 978 1 4152 0777 2 (ePub)
ISBN 978 1 4152 0778 9 (PDF)

Contents

Introduction

In 1981, I opened the first black law firm in Nelspruit, in the then Eastern Transvaal (today's Mpumalanga Province) with two friends and colleagues. Among the numerous cases the firm handled, I also represented members of the African National Congress (ANC) and its military wing, Umkhonto we Sizwe (MK, the Spear of the Nation). Consequently, in 1985 I was forced to flee my country of birth into exile. During my stay in Maputo, Mozambique, I became a regional commander of a unit of MK. This unit operated clandestinely, servicing political activists inside South Africa. It was a perilous task. The apartheid state used every means at its disposal, mostly illegal, to break the ANC. Exposure could result in detention, disappearance and even death. Members of my unit had to be extra vigilant; we were always on the move and in hiding. It is surprising that in spite of this I was able to find time to indulge in one of my favourite hobbies: writing poetry.

I first developed an interest in poetry when I was a teenager looking after my family's livestock in Polen, in the then Northern Transvaal (today's Limpopo Province). But I started writing when I was a student at Maripi High School (the name was changed to Orhovelani High after the introduction of the homeland system). Back then I wrote poetry in my indigenous language, SePedi (North Sotho). One such was 'Tjeketjeke', a poem about my grandmother's movement when she brought us food in the field where we were looking after the livestock or tilling the land with donkeys and cattle. When I went to the University of the North, popularly known as Turfloop, I wrote and read poetry in Afrikaans. This was new and unexpected. Due to apartheid, the majority of black South Africans associated Afrikaans with oppression. It was particularly the case in an environment where the black-consciousness philosophy was dominant. In spite of this, my poetry stimulated an interest among the students and was the highlight during the African Arts Week. Some of my poems, like 'Wie is ek in my land van geboorte?' ('Who am I in the land of my birth?'), were subsequently published.[*]

I wrote many poems in exile. Regrettably, archiving them was a luxury I did not have. *Chants of Freedom* is a collection of poems which, fortunately, made it back to South Africa after 1990. I became aware of the existence of these poems only this year, when I was researching for my biography. I felt it was imperative that they be published, including a couple I had penned recently. All the poems in this book are in English.

The poems in *Chants of Freedom* are a reflection of the various influences during the different times in my life. For example, I grew up in a rural area where we lived off the land and hunted to survive. 'This one is ours' speaks to that time in my life, a life that was disrupted by the government's policy of forced removals. Many black people were forced to become migrant labourers. I have vivid memories of my late father working as a teacher in the distant Lowveld villages. Before him, my grandfather worked in the diamond mines in Kimberley. 'Gold' illustrates the plight of migrant labourers in South Africa.

The poems also pay tribute to the role played by women and the youth in the liberation struggle. In 'The

---

[*] Mathews Phosa. *Deur die oog van 'n naald* (Cape Town: Tafelberg, 1996)

beautiful ones are now born', I show how the youth resuscitated the names of Nelson Mandela, Oliver Tambo and Joe Slovo, among others, and inspired widespread resistance across the country.

I finally took the decision to leave the country and go into exile after learning that one of my comrades, with whom I operated underground, had been detained and severely tortured to the point that he broke down and divulged some sensitive information to the police about my role. Such a comrade would generally be perceived as a sellout. In 'Comrade, you're not a traitor', I attempt to explain that we cannot afford to judge or condemn those we feel betrayed us and the struggle. We have to first try to understand the circumstances that caused them to respond in the way they did.

My 'chants of freedom' are distinct in their attempt to demonstrate that the political activists were human beings. They had feelings. Occasionally, feelings of uncertainty crept in, and quitting for some, if not most, seemed like the best option. Conversely, 'My share' attests to the unyielding belief among political activists that South Africa would one day be free and everyone would enjoy the fruits of democracy. This is what inspired peace-loving people to continue struggling in spite of the risks involved.

Finally, the poems in this book celebrate the victory over apartheid. They eulogise all those who contributed to the fight for democracy, black and white. They are a clarion call to all to work together to make South Africa a better country.

I want to acknowledge my grandfather 'Mochaka' and grandmother 'Tjeketjeke' for contributing so much to my upbringing; and my father and mother for ensuring

9

I received education, and for shaping my life. I want to thank my wife who stood by me before and during the difficult times of exile when she lived like a widow; for her unstinting support and love. I want to thank my four children – Moyahabo, Tshepiso, Mathlatse and Lesika – for being such a great inspiration and source of unending happiness.

MATHEWS PHOSA
APRIL 2015

Tears of blood

i can't stop my bleeding eye
for the wound is unfathomable
the stream overflooded
endless menstruation
i suffer life
in this dingy cave
seems pain is allocated to me
pleasure for others
the future pregnant with uncertainties
yesterdays are unpleasant to touch
the gush is unsightly and cries
tears of blood
i can't halt
the tide too overwhelming

Chicken-run

turning and turning
his thoughts about tomorrow
the future dark
and dampened
the metamorphosis
underwent by time
laying a burden on him
he, having it his way
what about offspring?
a cloud of uncertainty
hangs on
quitting is tempting
a short-cut answer
so the drainage
keeps flowing
some have given up
the chickens
on the run
turning and turning
his mind about tomorrow

Call me by my name

ask me who i am
a simple Azanian
uncomplicated
i need no introductions
no political birth certificates
    call me not
    Kaffir
    i'm no Native
    call me not Bantu
    i'm no Plural
    resist the temptation
    to call me co-operative
    call me by my name
    i'm an Azanian
    that's my name
    to which i'll respond

Standing ajar

with locked souls
they walk past me
refusing to let me in
only thrusting me with suspicious eyes
i crave to touch your spirit
yet it coldly shuns me
i knock on your hearts
i'm like you
made in His image
let me in
or come to me
the door of my soul stands ajar
for you to run in

Dreamland

here in my hovel
where i wrap myself
in blankets of sand
i wake up in the night
i chew and chew and chew
mca – mca – mca
yet there's nothing to swallow
i scream and scream and scream
'i don't want it!'
opening my mouth
attempting to state my side
but there's no voice to hear
i jump and jump and jump
yet i do not fall
here in my dreamland
where i shoulder
dreams of dreams
i scream and scream and scream
in my land of dreams
pretending to be independent

Negative education

innocent creatures
deprived of greatness
toddlers taught to hate
all that is black
to associate some with dinosaurs
intent on grabbing their poppies
detained in self-imposed ignorance
only knowing me as an enemy
heads drummed
with negative education
to hate me
only because
i'm black
yet i love you

Plunged in hell

you did it
the heaven for you
found on earth
what you desire
within the parameters
of your laws
you have
the heaven for you
on earth
you have
legislated my misery
living in plenty
to my exclusion
i scorch in fear
of your coarse hand
i cringe in horror
hearing your knock
in the heart of my sleep
having pitched heaven
you ensured i'm chained
chide me not for your felony
i'm plunged in hell
while you have
heaven on earth

Crossing the line

i've crossed the line
called on the other side
by whispering
familiar voices
only audible to my ear
beckoned by known hands
only visible to my eye
seem to see faces i remember
dum—dum—dum
open the churchyard gate
dum—dum—dum
it's me, it's me
i come naked
accompanied by dirges
to deliver me to you
i've served
i've come to rest

The winter of discontent

it was
a winter of discontent
the atmosphere
packed with horror
then i saw them
   worried faces
    bruised faces
    bloody faces
    swimming through fear
    and courage
fire! fire!
grrrr-grrrr ta-ta-ta
what could we say
we rejected a snake
in return we got a bite
funeral undertakers thrived
there was carnage
of the cruellest order
that was the day we said 'NO'
and donated our blood
a day of pain and depression
our hearts soaked in our tears
we buried them one by one
the nation was wounded
on that day
the winter of discontent
i'll never forget
to remember
grrrr-grrrr ta-ta-ta

The unsung heroes

the war is won
the German menace defeated
side by side we fought
to halt the flow of Jewish blood
peace, peace, peace
stream back home
the silent race is on
the relics of Hitler's booty
white heroes, here
i mean, here at home
some rewarded with free farms
our grandfathers – only bicycles
to ride home to the bush
on the lean ntlanya*
'fietse is goed vir hulle'
ride home, ride home
through the desert
ride home, ride home
denied their share of the booty
though you staked your life
side by side
on the hills
down the valleys
in the unknown lands
side by side you fought
without reward
i salute you

---

* ntlanya means a bicycle

Survival of the children

these children of the soil, are they sinking
picking up the gauntlet
they rise like the moon
peeping through dark clouds
to shed light on the dark earth

it's tough to be born black alive
the stillborns are lucky, i swear
those born alive are stifled
the racial hail hammering
yet, they survive!
the storms of harsh hatred

this madness is not going to stop
riddling infants with bullets
raking the nerves of the children
bang-bang they've had enough
picking stones
all in defence of their future
smirking they refuse
insisting on a spot under the sun

To the beloved comrades

victory is certain
victory is imminent
the enemy is committing error after error
no matter how invincible he may look
keep on keeping on
the road is too long
the struggle protracted
no matter the odds
be determined for the worst
beware of the impimpis
that stab you in the back
fear not the sellout
for their battle is lost
hang onto the iron belief
that this country belongs to all of us
spit in the face of all foreign ism
fight on for the war is raging
i love you, i revere you
internalise and intensify
mobilise the liberatory forces
to achieve democracy
to defeat the racists of this earth
who feed on hatred and prejudice
sting like a bee
demoralise the enemy
surrender he shall –
victory is in your hands

My share

wandering in the shadow of life
here i vow
to push this stone
and push it further
toward the edge of the precipice

here i swear
i'll have my share
of the sunrays
i'll have my share
of the moonlight

here i demand
the winks and smiles
from the stars

here i am
unsurrendering
violently non-violent
spewing out slogans of peace
'this is ours'
i'll have my share

Yoo-yoo sa'mma
(a praise song for our leaders)

le ya mmona Mandela (2x)
    yoo – yoo sa'mma (3x)
o paletse bo Vorster
    yoo – yoo sa'mma (2x)

le ya mmona Mbeki (2x)
    yoo – yoo sa'mma (3x)
o paletse maburu
    yoo – yoo sa'mma (3x)

le ya mmona Sisulu (2x)
    yoo – yoo sa'mma (3x)
o paletse bo-Strijdom
    yoo – yoo sa'mma (2x)
    yoo – yoo sa'mma (3x)

le ya mmona Mhlaba (2x)
    yoo – yoo sa'mma (3x)
o hlabile maburu
    yoo – yoo sa'mma (3x)

le ya mmona Mlangeni (2x)
    yoo – yoo sa'mma (3x)
o laile maburu
    yoo – yoo sa'mma (3x)
    yoo – yoo sa'mma (3x)

le ya mmona Kathrada (2x)
    yoo – yoo sa'mma
o paletse bo-Verwoerd
    yoo – yoo
    yoo – yoo sa'mma

hei … ta comrade Mkwayi – bri-bri
ta-ta comrade Motsoaledi
heita-ta-ta-ta

Let go Namibia

virgin land
plundered by swines
who mined to swell
their pockets full
they took the diamond
threaten to make the water fishless
every thing and all they took

enslaved by a galaxy
of predatory pigs
land maimed
a people murdered
by international piracy

parasitic masters
who salivate
itching to
ride, rape and rob
a tiny gallant nation
of people who never say die

let go Namibia
from Walvis Bay to Kunene River
just let Namibia go
viva SWAPO
viva comrade Nujoma
viva comrade Toivo ja Toivo
victory is certain

No other alternative

as the iron heel
of big Botha
continues to trample
on us
this is a declaration of war
a call to battle
the road to peace
is already soaked in
dams of blood and
    tears
in search of democracy
in the face of racial obstinacy
the only alternative
is to wage a war
the people's war
on all fronts
it's the only alternative
permitting no spectators

A poem for James Matthews

comrade James Matthews
once asked me to write a poem
about the Wounded Nation
that was in 1974
now is 1986
i still have not done so
i'm guilty of poetic negligence
i stand convicted
now i shall serve my sentence
the old guy was right
old James, you saw deep into it
it's an ever bleeding wound
spurting blood every day
every morning
we wake up to collect the maimed, dead
but did your small eyes see so far
yes old James
those wifeless fathers in hostels are bleeding
the husbandless mothers in the reserves
are bleeding
the workers down the shafts
the domestic servants
the factory folks
the farm workers
the students
everybody
all of us
we are bleeding
the apartheid sword
has cut too deep in us

The threshold

here we stand
with the black
    green and
    gold
flag in one hand,
with the red
    star
    hammer and
    sickle
flag in the other hand

here we stand
on the threshold
armed to the teeth
with the Freedom Charter
ready for implementation

here we stand
on the threshold
enshrined in our hearts
is social justice
    Freedom Charter and
    happiness
for all our people

Comrade, you're not a traitor

i heard you scream
as they smashed your head against the wall
it must have been painful
'leave me, leave me'
you shouted as they squeezed your testicles
the agony was captured in your voice
they told you they knew all
that we have all betrayed you
little did you realise they were lying
how could we have betrayed you
when we were not within their reach
we had taken cover in silence
so you told them all

comrade, we cannot judge you
never shall we condemn you
you are not a traitor

Our mothers march with us

how can the painful memory ever vanish
of the day our mothers said enough is enough
we are not paying apartheid rent
and paid instead the ultimate price

the long peaceful march of mothers
met with butchers
who rained bullets on them

the Southern Nazis have done it
we are looking for bodies to bury
please give us our dead
don't consign our mothers to secret graves

our mothers are with us
on this final onslaught
against the blood thirsty racists
bent on protecting the status quo
of raping our dignities
we shall march with our mothers
to the winning post of freedom

The carols crucified

if we can't sing our carols any more
by state decree
how do we
celebrate His birth

if we must bury our heroes in silence
when dirges are held suspect
how do we
pay them our last tribute

if services are banned
by police commands
how do we
continue to praise Him

if the price for truth is guillotine
by bullets of death-squads
how do we
continue

if the candle is snuffed
by military orders
how do we
see the way ahead

if we just can't sing our carols any more
oh, you tell me
why can't we sing our carols any more
oh, we want to sing our carols

Who killed Matthew Goniwe?

it's all swinish
machinations of rogues
recalcitrant racists
the enemies of justice
exorably married
to filthy intrigues

which rubicon did they cross
pooh! pooh!
'don't push us too far'
pooh! pooh!
powerdrunk murderers

Matthew Goniwe
was bludgeoned to death
he lies silently
in their secret grave
i swear, they know where

but Matthew is immortal
he now lives
in the soul of the masses
no, Goniwe shall never die
long live Matthew Goniwe

Not guilty

i'm only eight, my Lord
accused by our lawmakers
of intimidation
supposed to have
stopped workers
from going to work
my Lord i plead slavery
i say i'm innocent
but, my Lord
let me tell you
who is guilty
you, my Lord
your police sons
your government
and, my Lord
you as well
i have to prosecute
for persecuting me
with criminal laws
and this, i shall do
in the people's court
as it pleases his Lordship
may i be excused
from your charades

The expectant bachelor

there they are
married men
living in singles
scrotums swollen
with sperm
eleven months old
yearning for the dear ones
those forcibly dumped
in the dry corners
drinking from drought
these are fathers
those are mothers
we, mesmerised infants
in this antagonism
of existing non-existence

mama doesn't know
where to hide her face
nor how to explain
mama doesn't know
starved of literacy and love
how can she
enlighten us
of these life's permutations
whose head or tail
she sees not
though she lives
always in expectation
of an expectant bachelor

This one is ours

we hunted unhindered from this land
 ate
 drank
 unrestricted
 from our soil
 that was before
 the highway horse-riders
 the Bible carriers

this land belongs to us
 Hintsa Gaika
 can testify to this
 Shaka Dingane
 would tell you
 Moshoeshoe Mantatisi
 can bear witness
 Morolong Sekhukhune
 would corroborate
 Malebogo Ngungunyane
 would no doubt concur
that this one Souther than South
is ours
 Jan van Riebeeck was a mere visitor
 made a citizen by African high generosity

this one is ours
from the international sea waters
to the Limpopo
the Karoo to the South Coast
the beautiful people of South Africa
it's ours, it's us

Is this not

i am sorry to ask
is this not
a trial of the innocent
by the criminals

let me ask
is this not
the time to repossess
our land of birth
from colonial plunderers

i will ask
is this not
the moment
to seize power

if i asked
is this not
the hour for imperialists
to sign the surrender documents

i'm sorry to ask
is this not
the right minute
for all slaves to revolt

oh i've asked so much
for so long
without getting an answer
now: okay, i say and demand
down with imperialism
down with colonialism

The beautiful ones are now born

hau! – hau!
    ai – ai
    they walk
    the dusty streets of KwaMashu
    ai – ai
    the beautiful ones are born

hau! – hau!
    ai – ai
    they trot
    the muddy streets of Alexandra township
    .... have you seen the beautiful ones
    ai – ai
    ai – ai
    they canter
    the deep dark dongas of Crossroads
    the beautiful ones are born

hau! – hau!
    ai – ai
    they spit fire in the faces of sellouts
    these beautiful ones are now born

    ai – ai
    viva Mandela
hau! – hau!
    viva Tambo
    ai – ai
    viva Slovo
hau! – hau!
    the beautiful ones are born
    ai – ai
hau! – hau!

Let me scratch my back

i walk a desert
encircled by plenty
the edifice of the haves
arrogantly surrounding me
let me scratch my back

don't call me a terrorist
for marauding
and blasting your conscienceless soul
get off my neck
i want to scratch my back

i feel the weight of your yoke
relieve me of your prejudice
get off my back
let me scratch my back

i feel an excruciating pain
there is a festering sore on my back
ripe and racking
let the abscess sputter its nasty contents
i want to scratch my back

To whom it may concern

these things are happening
to whom it may concern
workers dying with drilling machines
in their empty hands
entombed deep down
others up the shaft

to whom it may concern
pupils smoked in teargas
this is the inferno
of the undustrialists
engulfing the others

these things we see
black children bleeding
and burning for freedom
the scoundrels digging deep
only concerned about lucre and lucre
the death of slaves only concern them
as far as it affects their balance sheets

we are concerned
about the waste
never do we care
about the debits and credits
for ever stand insolvent
no rights, no votes
nothing
it concerns us

She did not know

mama did not know
that i escaped like a rat
when the security police
hunted me to kill me

where is your son ... they asked
which one ... she replied
the lawyer terrorist ... they said

she shook her head and said
i do not know

for indeed mama did not know

they returned moons later

your son is dead – they told her
which one – she replied
i have two sons
bring me the corpse

i want to honour and bury him

show me the corpse – she demanded

she did not know
we were still alive
until she heard
from radio potato*
mama did not know

---

* radio potato is gossip

41

Gold

i'm right down in the belly of the earth
i mine you
i left my dear wife
and the little beautiful ones
in search of you
gold

i labour second by second
my body convulsing behind the drill
it's me chasing you through
every corner and crevice
deep deep down
condemned to artificial bachelorhood
gold

177 of my comrades died
swallowed by the fires of finance
young widows
young orphans
these, are your sad casualties
gold

you glitter in my gloomy face
i pick you, clean you
for others – the others
why not for myself
gold

the more i dig you
the more i stay poor
the more you shine
the duller i become
gold

you who cling
       on the necks
       on the arms
       on the ears
       of parasites
those who reap where they have never sewn
gold

money is your sweetheart
i see that, i have none
so you desert
to the hands of highwaymen
gold

your lustre shall never blind me
to the disproportional relations of things
you intensify my pangs
as you consign me
to a pensionless pension
gold

South Africa belongs to us all

We belong together – she belongs to us all
no whites will be exiled to the sea,
no blacks will be discriminated against ever

Hold hands dear brother
embrace good sister

Tomorrow beckons to us all
to rebuild and transform from the ashes of segregation
to a new edifice of non-racialism
she belongs to us all

Let us toyi-toyi quietly to a common future
one South Africa
one nation
one citizenship
one future

Boys and girls are back

Humbly claim your victory,
boys and girls are back,
looking into a treacherous tomorrow,
this is your time,
to make or to break.

Give us the spirit,
we need a virile soul,
give us a vision,
we need a tank of ideas.

Choose your side,
you can't be both
and everything,
to fish and swines.

Hard work is the seed,
to plant, to venture,
this is the final option,
for burgeoning nations,
wisdom is the watchword.

You call yourself a leader,
you close your ears,
shut your mouth,
open your eyes,
forward march!